DANNY DYNAMITE

JEAN URE

Illustrated by Martin Chatterton
and George Hollingworth

CORGI PUPS

Series Reading Consultant: Prue Goodwin
Reading and Language Information Centre,
University of Reading

DANNY DYNAMITE
A CORGI PUPS BOOK: 0 552 546003

Printing History
Corgi Pups edition published 1998

Set in 18/25pt Bembo Schoolbook by
Phoenix Typesetting Ilkley, West Yorkshire

Corgi Pups Books are published by Transworld Publishers Ltd,
61-63 Uxbridge Road, Ealing, London W5 5SA.
in Australia by Transworld Publishers (Australia) Pty. Ltd,
15-25 Helles Avenue, Moorebank, NSW 2170
and in New Zealand by Transworld Publishers (NZ) Ltd,
3 William Pickering Drive, Albany, Auckland.

Made and printed in Great Britain by
Cox & Wyman Ltd, Reading, Berks.

CONTENTS

Chapter One

This is the story of how Danny Dynamite stood up to the dreaded Billy the Skid and his gang of mountain bikers.

It all began on a warm summer's evening in August. Danny and his mates were out in the street, playing cricket.

Omar and Leanne were fielding

And so was Leanne's dog Toby

Russell was bowling

Clive was batting

and Danny was keeping wicket

The twins, Donna and Daisy,
were on the boundary. Rosie
the Rottie was with them.
Rosie belonged to the twins.
She was a great big slopbag.

Cats were everywhere, snoozing
in heaps on window sills, in
doorways, on the tops of walls.

Bodley Street was a good
street for cats. It was a good
street for children!

The sun was shining, the
birds were singing, and Clive
had just hit a six! A happier
scene it would have been hard
to imagine.

But wait! Just a short
distance away . . .

Chapter Two

Watch out! The bad guys are coming! Billy the Skid and his gang of mountain bikers are riding through the streets. The meanest bunch in town!

"Yeeeeee-**hah**!"

The blood-curdling cry echoed round the rooftops and bounced off the walls.

"Yeeeeee-**hah**!"

Once upon a time there was a playground chant which went like this:

Billy Skiddo and his men
Don't care how and don't care when.
Bash you, mash you,
Pulp you up and trash you!
Out to get you if they can,
Beware of Big Bill Skiddo Man!

Whole streets were cleared in seconds when Billy the Skid came riding through. Little children ran crying to their mums. Even big children didn't stop to argue.

Nobody argued with Billy the
Skid. He was the terror of the
playground. Now he was on the
warpath, so beware!

Billy Skiddo's come to town
With his men to do you down.
Out to get you if they can,
Beware of Big Bill Skiddo Man!

Meanwhile, back at Bodley
Street . . .

Thwack!

Straight into the churchyard!
Now what were they to do?
Who was going to be brave
enough to go and fetch it?

No-one liked going into the churchyard, even in daylight. It was dark and spooky, full of dead guys in their graves. Also, a girl at school had once told Leanne that there were ghosts.

Danny was just about to say
that he would go, as long as
the dogs went with him, when
there came the sound of an ear-
piercing shriek:
"Yeeeeee-**hah**!"

Everyone froze. Billy the Skid
and his gang of mountain
bikers had hit Bodley Street!

Chapter Three

Billy Skiddo's been and gone
See the damage he has done!
All that you can do is run,
Run from Billy Skiddo!

"I ain't gonna run!' said Clive.

"Me neither," said Russell.

"Gotta do something!" said
Clive.

But what?

"We could set the dogs on
'em," said Omar.

Not a very good idea. Rose
was a great big slopbag. She
even ran from spiders.

And Toby was too small.

"So what we gonna do?" said Daisy.

"What we gonna do?" said Donna.

It was Danny who came up with an idea. Danny's mum and dad ran a fruit and vegetable stall in the local market.

Danny said that what they
would do was start collecting all
the old squashy tomatoes and
pulpy oranges and slippy, slimy
cabbage leaves that his dad
threw out at the end of every
day.

"We'll keep 'em till they're
all stinky and gungy and when
the Skid comes back we'll pelt
him with 'em!"

"It'll make him awful
mad," said Omar.

Nobody listened to Omar.
Billy the Skid was a bully, and
you had to stand up to bullies.
Their teacher, Mr Biswas, had
told them so.

They were going to teach
Billy a lesson! When he came
back, he was going to be pelted!

Chapter Four

The days passed, and Omar
began to breathe a little easier.
Maybe Billy wasn't going to
come back. Maybe he had
decided to stop being a bully.
Miracles do happen!

But not this time.

The Skid!

The Skid!

And here they came, the
mountain bikers, with Billy at
their head.

"Quick!" cried Danny. "Get the gubbins!"

The gubbins was all the old fruit and veg that they had been collecting. They had kept it in a big plastic dustbin sack, and now it was all stinky and gungy and absolutely disgusting. And Billy was going to be pelted!

"I don't reckon they'll be
back in a hurry," said Clive.

Oh, but Clive was wrong!
Nobody threw rotting veg at
Billy the Skid and got away
with it.

Next morning, when Danny
and his mates came out to
play . . .

Billy woz Here. BE WARND

He didn't know how to spell,
but the message was clear.
"He's really mad," wailed
Omar.

The Skid was *hopping* mad.
He'd be back!

Chapter Five

Now what were they to do? They had tried standing up to the bully and it had just made him mad.

Maybe Mr Biswas was wrong. Maybe standing up to bullies was not what you should do.

That was what Danny's mum always said.

So what you gonna do Danny Dynamite!

Danny Dynamite

But Danny wasn't just going to sit back and do nothing!

"I'll think of something," vowed Danny.

And he did! Danny's mum
was quite right: you can't fight
violence with violence. But Mr
Biswas was right, too: you
have to stand up for yourself.

"I've got an idea!" cried
Danny.

It was a good idea, but he
would need someone to help
him.

Clive? Russell?

Omar? Leanne?

What about the twins?
The twins looked at each
other. Poor Rosie was under
the kitchen table and wouldn't
come out, and the twins were
seriously annoyed.

They nodded.

Down with bullies! Down with the Skid! Next time Billy came, they were going to be ready for him.

Chapter Six

A few days later . . .

By the time the gang came hurtling through, the street was empty — except for one small figure at the far end.

Danny stood there, hands on hips, blocking the path.

Billy's lip curled. Who did this little squit think he was?

"Get out the road!" roared Billy.

But Danny just went on standing there.

"If you don't go away and leave us alone," said Danny, "the Big Bad Bogeymen will get you."

Big Bad Bogeymen? Billy
threw back his head and gave
a great guffaw.

This silly little squit needn't
think he could scare Billy the
Skid with his soppy baby talk!

Danny stood his ground.
"This is our street," he said.
"You've got to behave yourself
if you come into our street."

Billy couldn't believe it! No-one
spoke to him like that! He
jumped off his bike and rushed at
Danny. Danny turned and ran.

Hot on his heels came Billy the Skid.

Clang! went the churchyard gate, as it slammed shut behind them.

No time to stop and look! Billy was going to get that little squit and teach him a lesson.

He was going to hash him, bash him, mash him to a pulp.

He was going to whack him, thwack him –

Danny put on a spurt. Heart hammering, blood pounding, he ran as he had never run before. Ran like the wind. Moved like dynamite!

He had to reach that far gate before Billy got him.

He made it – just! The gate banged shut in Billy's face.

Now Billy was locked in the
churchyard and couldn't get
out!

Lemme out of here!

He wasn't scared, of course.
Not he! Billy the Skid wasn't
scared of anything.

Except perhaps ghosts. If
there were such things. But
there weren't.

Were there?

Help! What was what? Over
there in the corner? Aaaaargh!

A white shape had risen from
one of the graves and was
coming straight for him. And
there was another! Like two
horrible maggots, gleaming in
the dusk.

Billy panicked. He hurled
himself at the gate and
scrabbled over.

The gang watched in
amazement. Could this be their
great leader? The great Skid?

"L-l-l-l . . ."

Billy pointed with shaking hand. The gang looked; their jaws dropped. The gate had opened and two glistening maggots could be seen sliming their way into the shadows. Ugh! Horrible!

The gang moved so fast
you'd have thought a herd of
rattlesnakes were after them.

Danny passed them on his way
back. Billy the Skid was grey
and shaking. What could have
happened? He must have seen
the Bogeyman!

And now the twins came
shuffling out through the
churchyard gate. They were
wearing two of their mum's best
pillowcases. The pillowcases had
had eye holes cut into them and
been daubed with silver paint.

Their mum was not going to
be pleased!

Or maybe she would be when
she heard the full story; how
Danny Dynamite, with a little
help from Donna and Daisy,
had stood up to the bullies.
How together they had defeated
Billy the Skid!

There is a new playground
chant now. It goes like this:

Billy Skiddo wets his knickers
When he sees a ghost that flickers.
He's afraid of bogeymen!
Runs off like a frightened hen!
Who's afraid of Bill the Skid?
No—one, after what he did!

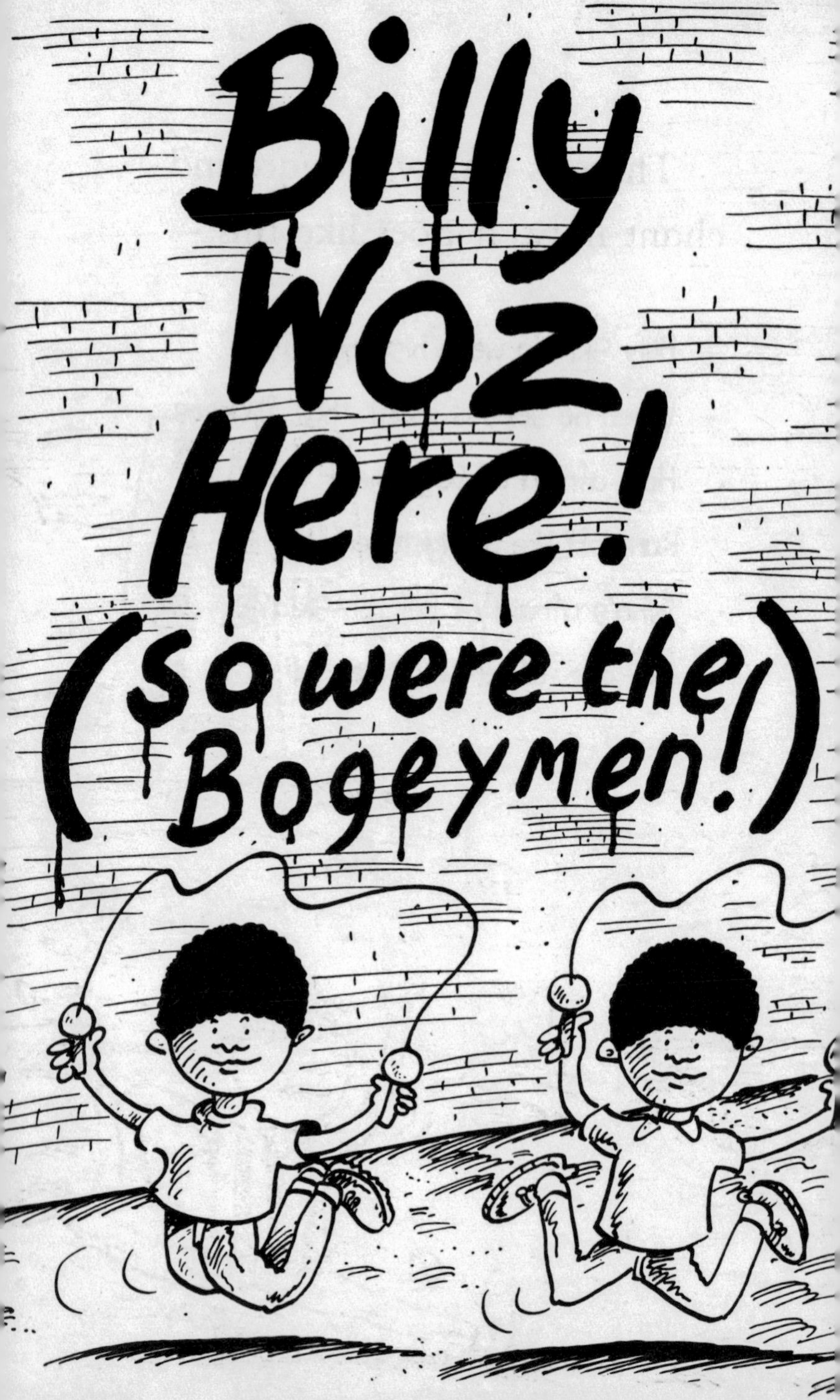
Billy Woz Here!
(so were the Bogeymen!)